ISBN: 0-7172-6495-5

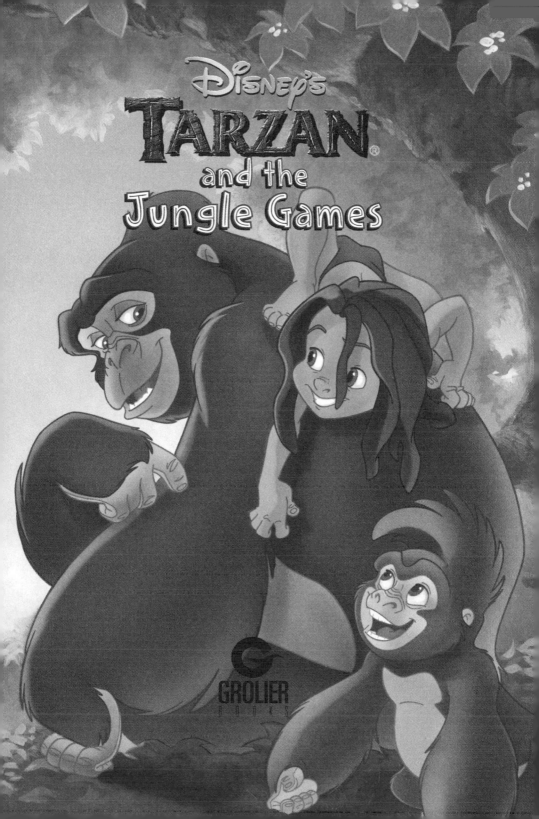

The sun was rising over the African jungle. Tarzan and his gorilla family were still fast asleep in the trees. But not for long.

Soon the warmth of the sun woke Tarzan and his gorilla playmates. They began to race down the tree. They were laughing and shouting and ready to play!

Kerchak, the leader of the gorillas, didn't like the noise. He still wanted to sleep.

So Kala, the kind gorilla who had become Tarzan's mother, hushed the playful youngsters. "Go and have breakfast in the coconut grove," she told them.

Tarzan and his best friend, Terk, quickly apologized. No one wanted to make Kerchak angry.

When they reached the ground, Tarzan and
Terk began to wrestle. The young gorilla giggled.
"Race you to the coconut grove," she shouted
to Tarzan and her other friends Flynt and Mungo.

When they reached the grove, Terk called, "Last one up is a rotten banana!"

Everyone quickly climbed up the trees.

"Got my coconut first!" Terk shouted with glee.

But when they were back on the ground, Tarzan examined his coconut and grinned.

"Hey!" he cried. "Terk might have the first one, but I found the biggest one!"

Terk didn't like that at all. "Hrumpf," muttered the little gorilla in disgust.

Then Mungo said, "Look at me! I opened my coconut first!"

This annoyed Terk even more. She couldn't stand hearing anyone bragging—anyone other than herself.

So Terk cracked her coconut on a tree branch above Mungo's head. Milk poured out all over him.

"Oops! Sorry," Terk said. "I just wanted to see if my coconut had the most milk."

Terk and the other gorillas began to argue. Tarzan sighed. Sometimes his friends spent so much time arguing that they forgot to play. He sat down and began to think.

Then Tarzan had an idea. "We're always trying to decide who is the best," he said. "Why don't we have a contest to decide who really *is* the best at everything? It could be fun!"

"All right," Terk offered, looking around.
"Why don't we try lifting these rocks to see
who's the strongest?" The young gorilla was
sure that this was a game she could win.

Terk was right. Tarzan especially had a
hard time lifting the rocks.

But Terk lifted hers with ease!

"Ha!" laughed Terk. "Who's the mightiest, strongest picker-upper in the whole jungle—?"

The young gorilla suddenly felt herself being lifted high into the air, stone and all!

"Me!" said a voice.

It was Tantor the elephant. He was the strongest of them all!

"What's the big idea?" snapped Terk after he put her down. "Can't you see we're in the middle of a game?"

Her angry words hurt Tantor's feelings. Tears filled his big elephant eyes. "I just wanted to play."

Tarzan felt sorry for their friend. "Of course you can play with us," he told young Tantor. "The jungle games are for everyone."

Feeling guilty, Terk agreed. "All right, I'm sorry. He can play, too."

So the five friends went off in search of a new game.

"Well, we've tried lifting," Tarzan pointed out. "What should we try next?"

Tantor spotted a little pond close by. He exclaimed, "Why don't we see whose nose can squirt out the most water?"

"Um, Tantor? We don't have trunks like you," Tarzan reminded him.

Then Tarzan came up with another
idea. He pointed to the pond. "Let's see
who's the best swimmer. We can race to
the other side."

Everyone liked the idea. The gorillas
immediately jumped into the water.

"YAHOO!" Tarzan called, jumping in with them.

Tantor couldn't wait
to join them. The young
elephant charged towards
the pond.

"Make room for me!"
he trumpeted, leaping
into the air.

"YIPPEE!" he yelled.

Unfortunately for Tarzan and the gorillas—and some fish—Tantor caused a giant wave!

"Watch out!" Terk cried. "Comin' through!"

Tarzan looked at the half-empty pond. "Well," he said, "I think we know who can make the biggest splash."

"Oops, sorry." Tantor blushed. "I think I hear my mother calling me. Uh, I'll see you all later."

"So much for that game," Terk snorted.

Tarzan just turned to Tantor and smiled. "We'll see you tomorrow," he said.

After drying off, the friends began looking for other games to play.

Tarzan scrambled up a tree. "Let's have a race," he suggested, pointing to a tree in the distance. "I wonder who can reach that old dead tree first."

"You know I'm the fastest runner in the jungle," Terk bragged. "But if you don't mind losing, let's go."

Tarzan didn't think he would lose. In fact, he was already smiling at the thought of a quick victory.

Everyone got into a starting position. Then Terk called, "Ready. Set—"

All of a sudden they heard a big CRASH behind them.

Suddenly a giraffe, zebra,
and rhinoceros bolted through
the bushes. The young animals
thundered past the four friends.

"Are they playing in our jungle games, too?" wondered Flynt.

"They don't look as if they're playing," replied Tarzan.

Suddenly the friends heard a loud ROAR!
They quickly turned to see a lion close behind them.

"I don't think *he's* playing either!" cried Terk.
"RUN!"

If they had been having their race, the rhinoceros would have won. She was the fastest runner. Tarzan jumped up on her back for a free ride.

"Help!" screamed the frightened friends.

Luckily, the young animals ran past
Kerchak, who was up in a tree. The huge
gorilla saw that the youngsters were in trouble.
He waited for the lion to pass under him. Then
he knocked him down with a mighty blow.
The lion fell to the ground with a THUD!

The other animals kept running. But Tarzan
and his friends turned around and walked slowly
back to Kerchak.

"Is he hurt?" Tarzan asked, peering at the lion.

"No," Kerchak told him. "But he'll wake up
soon. You'd better go before he does."

Tarzan and his friends thanked Kerchak for saving them.

"Wow," Terk sighed as they wandered away. "I'm glad we *all* won that contest!"

Tarzan nodded. "Some jungle games are more fun than others."

The other gorillas agreed.

So the friends rested, ate, and played until nightfall. Finally, it was time for them to return home.

They were tired and happy. And even Terk had learned that you didn't have to win a game to have fun playing it.

As everyone settled into their beds in the trees, Kala looked around and smiled. She whispered to Kerchak, "It seems the youngsters have worn themselves out playing their jungle games."

The huge gorilla nodded and said, "But I think they're having one last contest: Who can snore the loudest?"

Kala chuckled quietly. Then she cuddled Tarzan and they all drifted off to sleep.